Hannah's Winter of Hope

Hannah's Winter of Hope

JEAN VAN LEEUWEN

PICTURES BY DONNA DIAMOND

Phyllis Fogelman Books
New York

Published by Phyllis Fogelman Books
An imprint of Penguin Putnam Books for Young Readers
345 Hudson Street
New York, New York 10014

Designed by Stefanie Rosenfeld
Composed by Tina Thompson

Printed in the U.S.A. on acid-free paper

First Edition
1 3 5 7 9 10 8 6 4 2

LIBRARY OF CONGRESS CATALOGING IN PUBLICATION DATA

Van Leeuwen, Jean.
Hannah's winter of hope / Jean Van Leeuwen;
pictures by Donna Diamond.—1st ed.
p.   cm.—(Pioneer daughters)
Sequel to: Hannah's helping hands
Summary: In 1780 in Fairfield, Connecticut, Hannah worries about her brother
Ben, a colonial soldier being held prisoner by the British, and joins her family
in rebuilding their home and preparing for Ben's homecoming.
ISBN 0-8037-2492-6
1. Connecticut—History—Revolution, 1775-1783—Juvenile fiction.
[1. Connecticut—History—Revolution, 1775-1783—Fiction.
2. United States—History—Revolution, 1775-1783—Fiction.]
I. Diamond, Donna, ill.   II. Title.   III. Series.
PZ7.V3273 Hat 2000 [Fic]—dc21 99-35491 CIP

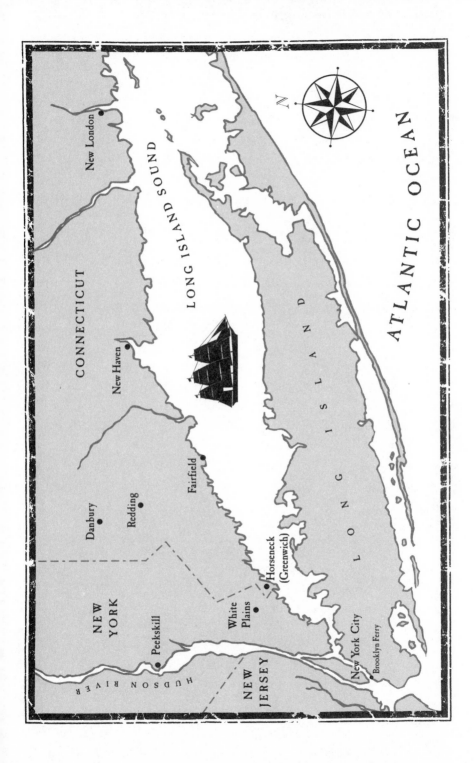

Chapter 1

It was snowing again. Looking out the window, Hannah could see fat white flakes swirling against a dark gray sky. It was always snowing, it seemed, this long, cold month of January 1780.

Inside, the fire crackled. Her older sister Rebecca's spinning wheel hummed softly. Mother's knitting needles made their comfortable *click-click-clicking* sounds. It should have been a cozy winter afternoon. But instead, Hannah felt squeezed-in and squirmy, like a wild animal caught in a trap.

It had been like that ever since winter started, since the family had to be inside so much, all crowded together in the one-room shed that had been Father's clock-making shop.

Oh, if only the British hadn't attacked last July and burned their house, Hannah thought for the hundredth time at least. She remembered its space, its rooms upstairs and down, its large attic hung with drying herbs and skeins of dyed wool. And the bedchamber she had shared only with Rebecca.

Father had tried to make the shed comfortable. There were straw pallets for beds. And a rough table and benches he had built to replace the furniture lost in the fire. Mother had hung strings of dried apples and herbs, and even made a curtain for the one window from a scrap of old grain sack. But still, there were six of them in one room, with hardly space to turn around without bumping into one another.

It made the boys, twelve-year-old Jemmy and seven-year-old Jonathan, quarrelsome. Father, always a serious man, frowned more than ever. Even Mother, who was so very patient, sighed now and then during these long winter months.

"Ow!" cried Jonathan suddenly.

"What is it?" Mother put down her knitting.

"Jemmy pounded me instead of the nail."

The boys were straightening nails gathered from the ruins of the old house. They would be reused in the new one Father was beginning to build.

"I didn't mean to," Jemmy said. "His hand was too close."

"Everything is too close," Jonathan complained.

Mother let out one of those little sighs that Hannah was getting used to hearing. "Why don't you boys go to the barn and see to the animals," she suggested. "It's nearly milking time."

"May I go too?" asked Hannah. How good it would feel to stretch her cramped legs.

But Mother looked at her with clear, steady gray eyes. "You know we must stick to our knitting, Hannah," she said firmly.

Hannah knew what that meant. Even now,

with so many houses in town burned, so many families struggling just to get through this hard winter, Mother was thinking of the soldiers. Soldiers like Hannah's oldest brother, Ben. They needed warm stockings and mittens. With the little wool she had saved from the fire, Mother meant to keep knitting for them.

"Yes, ma'am." Hannah poked her long needle into the wool again.

Just at that moment, a knock came at the door. Jemmy, standing next to it, pulled it open. Snow and freezing air came whirling in, and with it a boy.

He was tall, with shoulders as broad as a man's. Bright red hair peeked out from a snow-covered cap.

"Is this the home of Nathaniel Perley?" he asked.

Father set down the musket he had been repairing at his workbench.

"Come in," invited Mother. "Warm yourself by the fire."

The boy stamped snow from his boots and took off his cap. He rubbed his hands to warm them. His cheeks, Hannah saw, were as red as his hair.

"My name is Sam Eaton," he said. "Mr. Spooner, the storekeeper, is my uncle. I have come to live with him now that my mother is dead."

"Oh!" Mother caught her breath. "I am sorry."

"Yes, ma'am." Sam's blue eyes had sadness in them. "It happened suddenly. And my father died two years back. I have three older brothers, but they are all in the army. The reason I am here, Mr. Perley, is that my uncle told me that you are a clockmaker."

Father nodded. "That I am."

"My father was a clockmaker too," Sam said. "In New London. I would like to learn the trade as your apprentice."

Father was silent a moment. He always took his time thinking things over. Then slowly he shook his head.

"I am sorry," he said. "But I am not doing

much clock-making now. There is little call for such luxuries with our country at war."

"But—" Sam seemed to be struggling to control himself, to be polite. "With all respect, sir, some day this war will end, and clocks will be in demand again. My uncle told me that you plan to rebuild your house this spring. I am only fourteen, but I am strong. I could help you in exchange for teaching me."

The way he talked reminded Hannah of someone. Who was it?

Father seemed about to refuse again. Then Sam added quietly, "Please, sir. I want to follow my father as a maker of fine clocks."

In spite of himself, Father's usually solemn mouth bent up in a smile. "You are a determined young man," he said. "Very well. It is a bargain."

Sam's face broke into a wide grin. "Thank you, sir!"

"Now that that is settled," said Mother, "will you sit down and have some cider?"

But Sam shook his head. "I best be going,"

he said. "I have a long walk to get back to town before dark."

With another flash of a grin and a flurry of snow and wind, he was gone.

Ben. That was who he reminded her of, Hannah thought. Ben, so tall and strong and sure of himself. Ben, with his determination to be a soldier. Ben, with his wonderful grin that made everyone feel happy.

Where was Ben on this cold, snowy day? she wondered. Was he safe and warm? Or tramping through the snow in search of those British soldiers they called Redcoats? It had been four months since his last leave. Oh, how she missed him!

I will write him a letter tonight, Hannah thought. I'll write to him and tell him about Sam.

Chapter 2

The snow had finally stopped, after two days. The sky was clear blue. The sun shone so brightly that Hannah blinked as she stepped outside. It was still freezing cold, but she didn't care. She was going to town with Father today.

Ned, the big chestnut horse, was hitched up to the sled. His breath made steamy puffs in the frosty air as he stood patiently waiting. Then Father helped Hannah in, wrapped a heavy blanket around her, and got in beside her. He shook the reins, and they were off.

Ned stepped out eagerly. He seemed as happy as Hannah to be outside at last.

"Oh!" she burst out. "What a beautiful day!"

"That it is," agreed Father.

Everything seemed so different under its blanket of snow. The stone chimney, all that was left of their house, looked like a white-gloved finger pointing at the sky. The Wakefields' farm, next to theirs, looked tidy and pretty, the ruins of their house hidden by white. Drifts covered the road, and the stone walls had disappeared. Trees bent their shoulders under their snowy weight.

Father was silent as they rode along. So Hannah thought about what they would do in town. Once it would have been exciting to be going to Mr. Spooner's store. She would see her friend Betsy Spooner. And there was always so much to look at and special treats to buy, like raisins, shoe buckles, a bit of lace for Mother's sewing.

Now, though, money was scarce. Their Continental bills were hardly worth anything. Hannah remembered a story Betsy had told her. Her father had hidden a good many dollars between the rafters in the attic. Mice found them and chewed them into a nest. But her father hadn't been upset. "Let the mice have them," he said. "And the coins for couches. They are worth more to them than to me."

Father traded for the few things they needed. His clever hands could fix almost anything: watches, tools, the old spinning wheel he'd found in the barn. He had repaired Mr. Spooner's musket. In exchange, the storekeeper would give them molasses, salt, coffee, and maybe some nutmegs or cinnamon.

"Do you think we might get sugar today?" Hannah asked hopefully. They hadn't had any since November.

"Perhaps," said Father.

As they approached the store, Hannah saw many sleds. She waved to some of their neighbors. Everyone seemed glad to be outside after all the snow.

Inside, Mr. Spooner's store was bustling. It

had been roughly rebuilt since that terrible day when the British had burned every shop in Fairfield, and a hundred houses and nearly as many barns. Hannah breathed in the smell of new wood mixed with wet wool, leather, and a hint of cinnamon. She looked for Betsy. There she was with her mother behind the counter, measuring out spices. And there was Sam Eaton, his hair the color of fire, carrying sacks of flour.

"Good afternoon, Nathaniel."

It was Mr. Turner, the blacksmith. Father stopped to talk with him and a group of other men as Hannah stood listening. As usual, the news was about the weather and the war.

"This looks to be the worst winter in forty years," one man was saying. "I hear Black Rock Harbor is frozen half a foot thick."

"I had a pair of oxen buried in the snow yesterday," said another. "My son Isaac only found them by their breathing holes."

"One good thing, though," put in Mr. Turner.

"We can rest a little easier about the British. They are unlikely to attack in weather like this."

Hannah was glad to hear that. For years now the British had come at night in small boats from Long Island, stealing cattle, burning, and looting. In the morning they were gone. The raids kept the whole town on edge. At least this hard winter gave them something to be thankful for.

"Hannah!" Betsy Spooner was pulling at her sleeve. "It's so good to see you! I didn't think any of us were going to leave our houses this whole month."

Hannah smiled. It was true. It seemed like forever since she had seen anyone but her own family. Except for Sam Eaton. "Your cousin Sam came to see my father the other day," she said.

Betsy nodded, her blond curls bobbing. "I know. And your father won't be sorry he's taken him on. Sam is a hard worker. Oh, have you heard? There is ice-skating on Barker's pond. I think Mother may let me go tomorrow if the

shop isn't too busy. Do try to come, Hannah. It would be such fun!"

Ice-skating! Hannah loved to skate. Ben had taught her years ago, when she was only four or five. He had patiently picked her up each time she fell until, suddenly, she could do it. She remembered the exciting feeling of moving so fast and easily, gliding over the silvery ice.

But would Mother let her leave her knitting to go ice-skating? "I'll try," she promised.

"Can anyone tell me the way to the Perley farm?" a man's voice asked behind her.

Father turned. "I can," he said. "I am Nathaniel Perley."

The man wore the blue coat of a soldier, though it was frayed and ripped. "My name is Jeremiah Cobb," he said. "I am afraid I bring you some bad news."

No! Hannah shouted inside her head. Oh, no. Not Ben.

The soldier hesitated, as if he could hardly force himself to go on.

"Yes?" said Father, his voice as calm and steady as it always was.

"Your son Ben," the soldier said quietly, "has been captured by the enemy."

Chapter 3

What will happen now?

Hannah kept hearing the question inside her head. But no one was answering it.

Mother had gasped when they told her about Ben. The color had drained out of her face, and she had had to sit down. Soon after that, without saying a word or taking a bite of supper, she had gone to bed.

Now it was morning. Mother's face was as gray as the sky outside the window. She bent over the fire, dishing up bowls of cornmeal mush. But still she hadn't spoken. Father, too, sat silently at the table.

Jemmy, across from Hannah, shuffled his

feet loudly. He couldn't stand the silence either, she knew.

"Father," he said suddenly. "What is going to happen to Ben?"

Father picked up his spoon, then set it down. "Well," he said slowly, "you know that officers and ordinary soldiers are treated very differently. Do you remember when our General Silliman was captured last spring?"

Jemmy nodded. Hannah remembered it well too. He had been kidnapped by the British from his own home in the middle of the night.

"Officers like General Silliman are held under guard in private homes," Father explained. "If they are lucky, they are exchanged for captured British officers. That has not yet happened for General Silliman, but he is living comfortably. Ordinary soldiers like Ben, however, are not treated as well." Father's face looked grave as he went on. "They are thrown into abandoned buildings like the Sugar House, an old sugar refinery in New York City. Or held on prison ships anchored offshore." His voice grew quiet. "I have heard tales of hard conditions in these places."

He said nothing more, but took up his spoon and began eating.

Oh, Ben! In her mind Hannah could see him shivering in some tumbling-down building with no doors or window glass. No blanket to cover himself. No food to eat. She shivered at the thought.

Looking up, she saw Mother gazing at her.

"Although Ben is a prisoner," she said, "we must be thankful that he is still alive. We will pray for his safety. And have faith that he will return to us."

Mother always had faith that the best thing would happen. It was amazing. After breakfast she seemed herself again. She bustled about, cleaning up, sending the boys out for wood, then settling in with her knitting. *Click-click, click-click.* Her needles moved so fast, it seemed she must be planning to knit mittens for every soldier in the Continental Army.

And that afternoon she said, "We can't have you boys sitting here with glum faces. I believe it would do you good to get outside. Why don't you try out the skating on Barker's pond?"

Jemmy's and Jonathan's faces lit up.

"Mother—" began Hannah.

Mother nodded. "Yes, Hannah. You, too, if you like. And Rebecca."

But Rebecca shook her head. Hannah knew she hated the cold.

An hour later Hannah found herself standing at the edge of Barker's pond. The afternoon was freezing cold, with a hint of more snow in the air. Mother had insisted that she dress warmly. She wore a red cloak, just the color of the cardinal she saw sitting on a snowy bush. Under it she had on three layers of petticoats, her own and Rebecca's. To keep her hands warm, she wore mittens and a muff. And on her head she had her cap and, over it, a hood.

Hannah was warm. The trouble was, she could barely move. She felt like an overstuffed sausage.

"Can't catch me!" Jemmy went speeding across the ice, racing with his friend Sam Rowland. Captain, Ben's big brown dog, ran after them. Jonathan tried to keep up, but he fell, his arms thrashing.

Getting to his feet, Jonathan waved to Hannah. "Look!" he called. "I can do it!"

Hannah wasn't sure she could. She took a wobbly step, putting out her arms to steady herself.

"Hannah! You came!"

Betsy touched her hand. Hannah felt one of her skates go one way, the other skate another way.

"Oh!" she cried. And she sat down hard on the ice.

"Hannah, I'm sorry." Betsy's concerned face peered down at her. "I must have given you a fright."

Behind her, Hannah saw another face. Red hair under a blue knit cap, red cheeks. Sam Eaton.

"May we help you up?" he asked.

With Betsy on one side and Sam on the other, Hannah struggled to her feet.

"Come on," said Betsy, taking her hand. "Let's skate together."

They circled the pond. Step, step, glide. Step, step, glide. Slowly Hannah began to get the feel of skating again. She pushed her feet a little faster.

"We were so sorry to hear about Ben being captured," Betsy said.

Ben. Captured. For just a moment, Hannah had forgotten. She felt tears stinging her eyes. She blinked them away. But her eyes were so blurred, she couldn't see the ice ahead of her. Her skate caught on a bump, and down she went.

"Oh, how silly of me!" she said. And how silly Hannah felt, sprawled out on the ice. Sam came skating up to help her to her feet again. What must he think of her clumsiness?

"It was my fault," insisted Betsy. "I shouldn't have talked about Ben."

Whether it was thoughts of Ben or all those clothes she was wearing, Hannah couldn't seem to stop falling. She felt as if she were five years old instead of eleven. At least, she thought, her many petticoats kept her from landing too hard. Jemmy, across the pond, was laughing at her. And once, Jonathan came over, looking down at her with his serious, dark eyes.

"I could show you how to do it," he offered.

Each time she fell, it seemed, Sam Eaton was nearby to pick her up. And though he always had a cheerful smile, he didn't laugh or tease. She was grateful for that.

One time he told her a joke. "It's so cold today," he said, "it reminds me of a story my grandfather used to tell. When he was a boy there was a winter so severe that even people's voices froze."

"Really?" said Hannah. She couldn't imagine it being that cold.

"Then when spring came they thawed out, and the most amazing sounds filled the air."

Hannah had to smile. Sam really did remind

her of Ben. That was the kind of silly story he would tell.

Another time Sam said, "Don't despair about your brother. My oldest brother, Thomas, was captured and put in the Sugar House. But he escaped from the prison yard."

That was something Hannah hadn't thought of. Ben was clever and brave and strong. Maybe he, too, could fool the British and escape their prison.

A few snowflakes were coming down. As they touched her face, Hannah felt a little stirring of hope. Quickly she got to her feet and looked around for Betsy. There she was across the pond, helping her littlest sister.

Step, step, glide. Step, step, glide. Hannah skimmed along. She felt lighter, no longer weighed down. Faster and faster she went. She was really skating now, gliding over the smooth silvery ice. She couldn't fall.

"Betsy!" she called. "Wait for me!"

Chapter 4

Fine flakes of snow drifted by the window. It was still another stormy day. Hannah had been keeping count. So far this winter there had been thirteen snowfalls. And it was only the middle of February.

The shed was even more crowded than usual this afternoon. Sam Eaton had come to start his apprenticeship with Father. They sat, their heads close together, at Father's workbench. On the floor beneath it, Jemmy and Jonathan were straightening nails again. And arguing again.

"You aren't hammering straight!"

"Yes, I am! You just want to do all the hammering."

But today Hannah didn't mind so much. Because today Mother was making candles. And Hannah was going to help.

"Is the wax ready yet?" she asked.

"Not quite." Mother had her largest kettle over the fire. She had to melt the wax until it was just the right temperature for dipping.

Hannah took in a deep breath. How she loved the fresh smell of bayberry! Some people made their candles of tallow, the fat from hogs or cattle or sheep. They burned well, but gave off an unpleasant smell. Mother, though, always used bayberries. The bushes grew everywhere near the shore. Last fall, Hannah and Jemmy and Jonathan had gathered the tiny grayish-white berries. Mother had boiled them and collected the wax that floated to the surface. It was this wax that she was melting now.

Hannah and Rebecca had cut wicks the length of a candle and carefully straightened them. They tied the wicks onto long, thin wooden rods. There were eight wicks on a rod, so eight candles could be dipped at the same time.

"All right, girls," she said. "Do you have the wicks ready?"

"Yes, Mother," said Rebecca.

"Good. We can begin."

The two girls carried a rod over to where Mother sat. She dipped the wicks into the kettle, then brought them up. Hannah saw that a thin coating of wax now covered each one. She and Rebecca took the rod and laid the ends across the two benches Father had made. The wax would harden for a few minutes while Mother dipped the next batch.

They worked quickly. Soon the rods were lined up in a long row, and Mother was dipping the first candles again.

"They are starting to grow!" Hannah exclaimed.

She loved to watch the candles grow fatter with each dipping. Mother knew just how long

to keep them in the hot wax each time. And as they grew, their color changed. They started out a dirty gray-green. But slowly they got cleaner and greener until, when they were finished, the candles looked just the way they smelled: fresh and spicy green.

On this gray and snowy day they reminded Hannah that spring would really come.

"May I dip some?" Hannah asked hopefully.

As always, Mother shook her head. She wouldn't even let Rebecca, at sixteen, do the dipping.

"The fire and hot wax are too dangerous," she said.

Mother was always worrying about burns. Once, Hannah knew, Mother's skirt had caught fire from a spark that flew out of the fireplace. Luckily, Father had been nearby and had quickly put it out.

Dip, lift, and dry. Dip, lift, and dry. Candle-making had a rhythm to it, just like so many everyday chores. Like knitting and spinning and milking. Mother must have dipped those rods twenty-five or thirty times, Hannah thought.

Then, finally, the candles were fat and long and beautifully green.

"Twelve dozen." Mother looked pleased. "They will take us through the winter and beyond. That is a good day's work."

It *was* a good day's work, Hannah thought. Making light to take them through this long, hard, dark winter.

"And you've done a good day's work too," Father was saying to Sam. "You must have watched your father carefully and studied his tools."

"Thank you, sir." Sam's face was as serious as Father's.

"We will continue next week."

"Those candles sure smell good." Suddenly Sam was smiling at Hannah, looking down at the rows of drying candles.

Hannah felt her face flush, though she didn't know why. "It's the bayberries," she mumbled.

"Well," he said, "I best be getting back to town. Good afternoon, everyone."

Opening the door, he nearly bumped into someone outside.

"Mr. Perley."

A young man stepped through the door. He was tall, but scarecrow thin. His worn coat hung from his shoulders as if it had been made for a much larger man. And though he was probably not yet twenty, his eyes looked old.

"Yes?" said Father.

"Do you not know me, sir?"

Something about his face seemed familiar to Hannah. But she couldn't quite place it.

"I am Josiah Plummer," the young man said.

Josiah Plummer! He was a friend of Ben's. He had enlisted in the army just before Ben had. But he looked so different than she remembered.

"Josiah, of course," said Father. "Forgive me. Come in, please."

Hannah and Rebecca hurried to move the candle rods so Josiah could sit next to the fire.

"Will you have some warm cider?" Mother asked.

Josiah nodded, looking grateful. "Thank you, ma'am."

He was shivering, Hannah noticed. Even after sitting by the fire for several minutes, even after Mother handed him a mug of warm cider, his hands kept shaking.

"Are you well, Josiah?" Mother asked, her eyes concerned.

"I've had a fever," he answered. "And frost-bitten feet. Mother wanted to keep me in bed, but I had to come. I have news of Ben. Three days ago I escaped across the ice with four others from the old Jersey prison ship. Ben is being held there."

"Oh!" Mother's hand flew to her mouth.

Hannah looked over at Father. His forehead wrinkled in a slight frown.

What kind of news was this? she wondered. Good or bad? It was good to know where Ben was. But what sort of place was the old Jersey prison ship?

Father cleared his throat. "How are conditions on board ship?" he asked.

Josiah hesitated, looking down at his mug. "I am afraid, sir, that this is not for the ears of ladies," he said.

"We are all Ben's family." Mother's voice was soft but firm. "You may speak freely."

Josiah looked at Father. He nodded.

"The *Jersey* is an old sixty-four-gun ship," Josiah began. "She is anchored off Long Island just east of Brooklyn Ferry. Because of her age, she is unfit to sail. Her masts and rigging have been stripped away, so nothing is left but a terrible, black, rotting hulk. And on board, life is just as bad."

Now it was Mother whose hands were shaking. She clasped them tightly together. "Go on," she said.

"Prisoners are crowded so tight below decks that they can hardly stand. At night they are in complete darkness, without a candle. They are fed thin oatmeal and moldy biscuits, and once in a while a bit of pork. Sometimes they are given bran cakes made to feed horses. And sometimes, for days at a time, they get nothing at all."

"There must be sickness," Father said.

Josiah nodded. "Every kind you can imagine. I saw yellow fever and smallpox and other diseases I didn't know the names of."

Yellow fever. Smallpox. Those were terrible diseases, Hannah knew.

"But for all the months I was there," Josiah went on, "no doctor ever came on board. The British do not seem to care how many die. To them, we are traitors who deserve any evil that may come to us."

Hannah could hardly believe her ears. All this sickness and no doctors? How could anyone be so cruel? And her brother was in this terrible place.

"And Ben?" Mother said quietly. "How is he?"

Josiah shook his head. "I don't know. He was brought on board the day before I escaped. I saw him for only a moment, and we couldn't speak. But he didn't appear to be ill. Just ragged and starving like the rest of us."

Mother closed her eyes. "Thanks be to God for that."

"That is all I can tell you," Josiah said. "I'm sorry."

"We are grateful to you for coming," Father told him. "And now I suggest that you go back to your warm bed and take care of that fever."

"Yes, sir." Josiah rose slowly to his feet. He looked worn out, and his hands still shook as he drew on his coat. But at least he was home now, Hannah thought, with a warm bed to go to.

As soon as Josiah left, Father took down his Bible.

"We must all pray," he said. "We must pray for Ben's safety. And for our own strength in the days to come."

Chapter 5

Hannah had terrible dreams. In one, Ben lay shivering on the floor. Nothing, not the fire nor piles of blankets nor Mother's hot drinks, could make him stop. In another, she heard Ben's voice calling her name. It seemed to come from across a vast sea. Hannah, on shore, searched and searched. Try as she might, though, she never could find him in the dense gray fog.

She told her dreams to Captain. The dog laid his big head on her knee as she talked. "Ben is going to get out of that place," she told him. "He will escape like Josiah did and come back to us. You'll see."

Captain wagged his tail as if he agreed.

But the days went by, and they heard no more news of Ben.

One morning Hannah woke up shivering. The fire has gone out, she thought sleepily. At night Father always raked the coals and carefully covered them with ashes, so as to save a bit of fire for morning. Then Mother would stir them up and add more wood to cook breakfast.

Opening her eyes, Hannah saw Mother poking at the coals, trying to get them burning. It was no use. The fire had gone out.

"Jonathan," she said. "Will you run over to the Wakefields' and get us some coals of fire?"

Jonathan crawled out of his blanket and quickly dressed. Mother handed him a small shovel to carry the coals, and he hurried off.

It was too cold to get up, Hannah thought. She would wait until he came back. She huddled close to Rebecca and tried to sleep.

But Jonathan did not come back. One by one, they all rose from their beds and sat wrapped in blankets, waiting.

"What could have happened?" Mother worried out loud.

"Shall I go look for him?" Jemmy asked.

Father nodded. "Perhaps you should, Son."

While Jemmy was gone, Mother brought out some johnnycake left over from last night's supper and a jug of cider.

"I'm afraid we will have to have a cold breakfast today," she said.

A few minutes later the door burst open. In came Jemmy, followed by William, the Wakefields' oldest son. William carried Jonathan in his arms.

"Oh, my!" Mother jumped up. "What is wrong?"

"There has been an accident," said Jemmy.

"Jonathan burned his hand," said William, "on the hot coals."

Jonathan's left hand was wrapped in a piece of rag. Hannah could see that he was in pain. His face looked pale, and he was trying hard not to cry.

"Put him down by the window," Mother told

William, "so I can see what the burn looks like."

Gently, William set Jonathan down on a bench next to the window. Mother began to unwind the rag.

"I'm sorry, Mother." Jonathan's voice quavered as he looked up at her.

"Hush," she said soothingly. "You have nothing to be sorry for."

"I got the coals of fire," he explained, "and started home. B-but then I tripped, and the coals slid off the shovel and burned me."

"I saw Jonathan from our window," added William, "and ran out to help."

William was such a kind young man, Hannah thought. He never talked much, but he was gentle and steady and hardworking. Rebecca thought so too. For the past few months they had been paying special attention to each other when they met at church or in town. Hannah thought they were courting. Glancing over at Rebecca now, she saw that her face was flushed and she was smoothing back her hair.

"Thank you, William." Mother had the rag unwound. "Oh, dear," she sighed. "The skin is badly blistered. We must make up a poultice to put on it."

"I can help," offered Hannah.

"Let me think." Mother frowned. "How did Granny Hannah treat burns?"

Hannah knew just where to look. In the small leather-covered box where Father kept his Bible was a thin pile of pages sewn together with thread. This was her grandmother's book of cures. Granny Hannah had known so much about herbs and medicines. That was because she was a midwife, a woman who delivered babies and also cured illnesses. Hannah had been thinking a lot about Granny Hannah lately. When she grew up, she'd decided, she wanted to be just like her.

Burns. Where had she seen Granny Hannah's cure for burns?

Hannah's heart thumped as she turned the pages. She had cured an injured sheep last spring using one of Granny Hannah's remedies. But this was the first time she might be able to help heal a person.

Jonathan moaned. He lay on his pallet now, with Mother beside him. Father, meanwhile, had finally gotten a fire going by striking a flint and steel together to make a spark.

"Mother, I've found it!"

Mother came to Hannah's side. They both struggled to make out Granny Hannah's tiny, faded writing.

"Beech leaves," said Mother. "Yes, now I remember. Jemmy, Hannah, and Rebecca, I want you to take buckets from the barn. Dig in the snow beneath the beech tree. Bring as many leaves as you can find. Hurry!"

"Yes, Mother." Jemmy went racing out the door before Hannah could even find her cloak and mittens.

"I will help too," said William.

On their hands and knees, they all dug in the snow like burrowing animals. Captain ran around, barking, then started digging too.

Hannah felt like the squirrels she often saw digging for nuts. Only there was more than a foot of snow, and it was packed down and crusted with ice.

"It's so hard," Jemmy complained.

"I know what we need," said William. He went to the barn for a shovel. In a few minutes he had dug out several holes.

Jemmy dove into one of them. A moment later he came up, a handful of leaves clutched in his mitten. "I found some!" he cried.

Hannah plunged into another hole. Soon she was covered with snow. She felt cold and wet from her cap all the way down to her shoes. Looking at the others, she saw that they all had frosty white coats and red faces. But they had collected two full buckets of beech leaves.

"I'll take them to Mother," she said.

The shed felt wonderfully warm to her now. And Mother had water already boiling in an iron pot.

"Good," she said.

They dropped in the beech leaves, and Mother began stirring the pot with her long wooden spoon.

Hannah watched very carefully. She wanted to make sure she would remember how to do it.

Mother stirred the leaves for a long time, until they had boiled down to a thick mass. Then she brought some up and spread it onto a thin cloth.

"Jonathan," she said, "this will help you feel better." She placed the poultice on his injured hand.

"It still hurts," he said after a moment, blinking back tears.

"I know," Mother answered. "It will keep hurting for a while. But you have been very brave."

The poultice had to be changed every hour, all day long.

"May I do it, Mother?" asked Hannah.

"Certainly, Little Granny," Mother said with a smile.

Hannah changed the poultices as gently and carefully as she could. Each time she did, Jonathan looked up at her with his big, dark eyes.

"Thank you, Hannah," he said softly.

He trusts me, she thought.

By evening, he was even smiling a little. "It doesn't hurt so very much," he told her at supper. "I think I am better."

Those were the very best words Hannah could hope to hear. She felt a warm, happy glow spreading throughout her whole body. So this was what it was like to heal people. Oh, she did want to be just like Granny Hannah some day!

She had an even better feeling the next day, when old Doctor Whitmore came to look at Jonathan.

"A bad burn," he said to Mother. "It will take time to get better. But it should heal nicely, thanks to your quick treatment."

"My daughter Hannah applied the poultices," Mother told him.

The doctor reached out and took one of Hannah's hands in his large, careworn ones.

"Good work, young lady," he said.

Chapter 6

Little by little, day by day, Jonathan's hand got better. Before long he could begin to use it again. And soon he was doing almost all the things he used to do.

Little by little, too, winter lost its icy hold on Fairfield. The snow, which had covered everything, shrunk to piles and then to white spots here and there. Ice turned to water, *drip-drip-dripping* off the roof of the shed. The ground thawed so that coming in from the barn, Father's and the boys' shoes were always covered with mud.

Spring was coming. Hannah could feel it in the March air.

The British must have felt it too, for the raids started up again. A mill was burned. Four cows were stolen from a farm just down the road.

Father's face wore its worried look once more.

"You must keep a sharp eye on Hattie," he warned Jemmy.

Hannah knew how important Hattie was to them since their other cow, old Bessie, had died last fall. Without Hattie, there would be no milk or butter or cheese for the family.

"I will," said Jemmy. "And so will Captain. He wouldn't let any strangers near our animals."

The best thing about the coming of spring was that soon Father could begin work on rebuilding the house.

Each time Hannah looked at the pile of wood stacked near the old foundation, she couldn't help feeling excited. The trees had been chopped down early in the winter. Father and Jemmy had worked hard taking off the bark, then squaring the sides of the huge logs.

They had dragged them from the woods on a logging sled pulled by Ned. Since then, the wood had been drying out and waiting for warmer weather.

At last came a day when the sun melted the last of the snow into puddles.

"Tomorrow," said Father at supper, "if the weather holds, I believe we can start work on the house."

Tomorrow!

Hannah could hardly wait for morning to come. She was awake before the sky began to lighten. She watched the window as black turned slowly to gray. Please don't let it rain today, she thought. Or, even worse, snow. When she saw the first pale rays of sun, she smiled with relief.

Right after breakfast, Sam and William came to help. Hannah was happy to see Sam's now-familiar grin, so wide that it seemed to go all the way to the edges of his face. Was it just because he reminded her of Ben? she wondered. Or was she starting to like him in a different way?

Everyone stood around that great pile of wood. "The first thing we need to do is sort the timber," Father explained, "and check for any damage. Then we will choose the strongest pieces for the sills and saw them to size. Sam, you work with William. Jemmy will work with me."

"And me too?" asked Jonathan. "My hand is better, so I can help."

Father smiled at him. "You too."

"What can I do?" Hannah asked eagerly.

Father turned to look at her. "This is not women's work, Daughter," he said gently but firmly. "You must stay inside and help your mother."

Hannah was so disappointed, she felt tears filling her eyes. Slowly she walked back to the shed with Mother and Rebecca.

Mother touched her shoulder. "You will be helping," she said softly, "by making a good hearty meal for the men when they rest at noon. I have in mind an oyster stew. Come now, we have much to do."

All morning Hannah worked side by side with Mother. She churned butter until her arm ached. She crumbled crackers for the stew. But all the time she was working, she was grumbling inside. Women's work! It wasn't fair. The butter she made and the crackers she crumbled would soon be eaten and gone. But the house the men were building would stand for years. Maybe a hundred or more. She so wanted to be part of that building!

At noon Mother served up the stew in steaming bowls. Father, William, Sam, and the boys crowded around the small table, eating and talking and laughing.

"Did you see the size of some of those timbers?" Jemmy asked. "They must be at least a foot across."

"They will make a sturdy sill for a house to rest on," agreed William.

"Didn't I help a lot by picking up wood chips?" Jonathan's eyes shone. He was feeling grown-up at being included among the men, Hannah could tell. Once more she felt a little pang of jealousy.

"You certainly worked hard," said Father. "We all did."

William had managed to sit next to Rebecca. Hannah watched them talking quietly together. Both had identical small smiles on their faces. Yes, she thought, they really were courting.

"Thank you, ma'am," said Sam as he finished his second helping. "That was the best oyster stew I've had since—" He stopped. "Well, it is as good as my mother used to make."

Jonathan put down his spoon.

"I'm ready to work hard some more," he said, and everyone laughed.

Hannah felt a little better. Even though she wasn't working on the house herself, she *was* helping those who were. That was something.

As she tended to her knitting that afternoon,

she listened to the raspy sound of sawing. Now and then, she stole little peeks out the window. There was the saw in Father's hands, its blade shining in the afternoon sun. Sam and William bending and lifting, carrying the long pieces of wood. And Jonathan darting about, picking up leftover bits for the fireplace.

The sun was growing low when the sawing finally stopped. Jonathan came in the door, his arms full of kindling, his face dirty but smiling.

"Father says come and see!" he said.

Hannah and Mother put down their knitting, and Rebecca stopped her spinning. They followed him outside.

Laid out on the ground were four huge timbers, the length and width of the old foundation. They were all squared and smoothed, ready to be placed on top of the foundation stones.

"These are our sills," Father told them, pride showing in his face. "Stout white oak, strong and sturdy. This is what our new house will rest on."

New house! The thought made Hannah smile. She could picture it inside her head: a fine, sturdy new house rising right here where the old one had stood. And Father had promised it would be even larger and finer than before.

Tired as they were, they all were smiling. Jemmy and Jonathan, William and Sam, and most of all, Father.

Those favorite words of Mother's popped into Hannah's head: "A good day's work."

As if Mother could read her mind, she smiled too.

"That was a good day's work," she said.

Chapter 7

Every fair day now, they worked on the house. Father and the boys, Sam, and sometimes, if his father could spare him, William. And every night, Hannah asked questions.

"When will the roof go on?

"How long will it be until we can live in the house?

"How do you know it won't fall down?"

Father shook his head, though his eyes were smiling. "My, my, Daughter," he said. "You want to know everything."

That was why Ben used to call her Goosey, that silly old nickname. He said Hannah was always poking her little beak into things.

But Father patiently answered all of her questions.

"To build a house," he said, "you first need to put up a strong skeleton. All those timbers out there will form the skeleton, or frame, of the house. After we've done the framing, then the roof and sides will go on."

"The frame is like the bones?" Hannah said.

"Exactly," answered Father. "I can't say how long it will take to finish. Many months, at least. We cannot work on it all the time, as soon there will be crops to plant. But I hope we will be living in our new house by next winter."

If only Ben were here, Hannah thought with a pang. Then the building would go much faster. And Daniel. Poor Daniel, William's younger brother, had joined the army with Ben and died of a fever at Valley Forge. Oh, Ben, she thought. Hang on. Be strong. Come home to us.

Hannah kept watching the building from the window. The frame was being laid out and joined together in sections on the ground.

After each section was finished, it would be lifted up and set on top of the sills.

One morning at breakfast, Hannah heard Father talking to Mother. "Do you think you could spare Hannah today?" he asked.

"Why, yes," replied Mother. "I think I could."

"Good," said Father. "I have a job for her."

A job for her! Hannah could hardly believe it. She was going to work on the house after all.

But when she found out what her job was to be, Hannah's heart sunk with disappointment.

"These are the tools we use for framing," Father explained. "When one of us needs a tool, you will hand it to him."

He told her what each one was called. Chisel. Mallet. Auger. Drawknife. Froe. Level. Keyhole saw. What strange names, Hannah thought, and strange shapes too. What did all those tools do? she wondered.

She didn't dare ask any questions now, though. Father was too busy to answer. And soon she was too busy to ask.

"Mallet!" called William.

"Level!" barked Father.

"Auger!" cried Jemmy.

Hannah hurried back and forth, from one to another, all morning long. At noon she was glad to rest. And even gladder to be sitting with the men for dinner instead of serving them. She might have the lowliest job, she thought, but at least she was working on the house.

It was mid-afternoon when Sam called, "Chisel!" Hannah watched as he used it to cut a rectangular hole at the end of a piece of wood. Finally, she decided, there was time for a question.

"What are you doing?" she asked.

"We join the frame together without using nails," Sam explained. "The end of another timber will be shaped to fit into this hole."

Just then Mother brought out some cider, and they all stopped to rest.

Sam sat down under the pear tree. "Have you

had any more word of your brother?" he asked.

Hannah shook her head. "Not since Josiah told us about the prison ship."

She hesitated, wondering if she should tell him about her latest dream. She hadn't told anyone, not even Captain. What if Sam made fun of her?

But he seemed so easy to talk to that she found herself saying, "Last night I dreamed that Ben escaped from the prison ship. He flew home on the back of a seagull."

Saying it out loud, it seemed silly. But Sam didn't laugh, or even smile. "I've had dreams like that," he said.

Whenever Hannah thought of that dreadful prison ship, she felt anger bubbling up inside her. "How could the British treat their prisoners so cruelly?" she burst out.

Sam's jaw tightened. "I don't know," he said. "Sometimes I get so angry, I want to run off and fight them like my brothers did. My uncle says I am too young to enlist. But I'm tall and strong and I can shoot a musket." He stopped. Then, so quietly that no one else could hear, he said, "I want to be a seaman like my second brother, Charles."

He talked just like Ben used to, Hannah thought, in the months before he joined the army. Something in his eyes, too, reminded her of Ben. And now look where Ben was.

"Listen to your uncle," she said, just as quietly. "Don't go."

Then Father was on his feet and calling her. "Hannah, bring me the large mallet, please."

They worked until the shadow of the old chimney grew long on the ground. Finally, Father set down his mallet.

"That is all we can do today," he said. "Jemmy, clean the tools and put them away in the barn."

"Mr. Perley, sir!"

Hannah turned to see a large Negro man with a round, pleasant face. She knew him from town, though she couldn't think of his name. A name from the Bible, it was.

"My name is Moses," the man said. "Used to belong to Mr. Thatcher, till he set me free. I been living over in Horseneck since then. I have news of your son, sir."

Oh, no! Hannah's heart jumped into her throat. Each time someone brought news of Ben, it was worse than before. She couldn't stand to hear it.

But Moses was smiling. "It's good news, Mr. Perley. Mighty good! I seen your son in Horseneck, and he is on his way home."

It took a moment for the news to sink in. Then, suddenly, they were all smiling. It was like the sun coming out after a long rain. Jemmy gave a cheer, and Jonathan jumped up and down. Hannah felt as if her heart would burst with joy.

"Please come inside," said Father.

Hannah would never forget the look on Mother's face when they told her.

"Ben? On his way home?" Clasping her hands together, she looked upward. "Oh,

thanks be to God!" Tears went rolling down her cheeks. Hannah knew, though, that they were tears of happiness.

As soon as she recovered, she invited Moses to sit down and rest.

"Thank you, ma'am." Moses looked grateful. He must have been walking all day, Hannah realized. Horseneck was about twenty miles away.

"How is Ben?" asked Father.

The smile left Moses' face. "Poorly," he said.

"Sick and starving, like all them that was prisoners. They set them free to walk home, but some will never make it."

Now Mother looked alarmed.

"Not your boy," Moses added quickly. "Least he didn't look to have the smallpox. Just so weak he could hardly stand. I left him with another soldier from these parts, sitting on a stoop outside a tavern."

Father stood up. "I must leave right away to find him," he said. "Jemmy, saddle up Ned."

"Beggin' your pardon, sir." Moses spoke up again. "It might be best to wait till morning. No telling where he may be now. No use trying to find him in the dark."

Father nodded. "I suppose so," he agreed.

Mother invited Moses to have some supper, but he refused.

"Thank you, ma'am," he said, rising wearily to his feet. "But I need to go tell that other boy's family."

"At least take some bread and cheese,"

Mother urged. She wrapped up a small bundle and handed it to him at the door.

"How can we ever thank you?" she said.

Once more Moses' broad face split into a big smile. "Don't have to thank me for nothing," he said. "Aren't I a free man?"

Chapter 8

Father left before dawn the next morning. Though Jemmy and Jonathan both pleaded to go with him, he took only Captain.

"I can travel faster alone," he said. "You boys help your mother prepare for Ben's homecoming."

Ben. Homecoming. Hannah could hardly believe it. She would be seeing her oldest brother before the day was over!

If Father found him, she corrected herself. *If* he was really all right.

Mother, she noticed, seemed to have caught the smiling fever. Hannah couldn't remember when she had looked so happy and excited.

She set them all to work, running here and there.

"Jonathan, go over to the Wakefields' and tell them the news. See if they have an extra blanket. Oh, and Ben is going to need clothes too, if William or Mr. Wakefield have any to spare."

Jonathan scurried off.

"Jemmy, we'll need to make up a bed for Ben close to the fire. Bring in a good pile of clean straw from the barn."

Jemmy raced outside.

"And girls, we are going to fix a special meal. I believe that Ben's homecoming calls for us to kill that last goose."

Once there had been a whole flock of geese pecking about the yard. But when the British had come and burned the house, they had stolen all but two. Mother had cooked one for dinner on the day of thanksgiving last November. Now there was just one left.

Hannah nodded. If ever there was the right time to cook that last goose, it was for Ben's homecoming.

"And a cake too," said Rebecca. "You know Ben loves cake."

"Oh yes!" cried Hannah. "Cider cake is his favorite. Could we make one?"

Mother smiled. "I think we could. Let me see, do we have everything we need? I believe we do. Except for the currants."

As soon as Jemmy came in, she sent him out again, to try to find currants at Mr. Spooner's store. Then Mother set the oven to heating. Rebecca began grating nutmegs, while Hannah powdered the sugar.

It was hard work. Sugar came from the store in hard cones. First Hannah had to break off pieces, using sharp cutters. Then she pounded the pieces until they crumbled into small bits. And finally she sifted them till they became fine as powder.

All the time she worked, Hannah thought of Ben's face. How he would smile when he saw that they had baked him a cider cake!

Just as she finished, Jemmy came back with the currants.

"Mr. Spooner didn't have a whole pound," he said. "Only half."

"Then half a pound will have to do," said Mother.

Soon the currants had been stirred into the batter, and the cake was ready for the oven.

"Now for that goose," Mother said.

It was Jemmy's job to kill the goose. Hannah hated to see any of their animals killed, even for such a special meal as this. At least she could say good-bye to it, she thought.

She followed Jemmy outside.

"Where is that pesky goose?" he muttered.

It wasn't in the yard with the chickens. Or around behind the barn. Or over where the garden used to be. Where was it?

Hannah and Jemmy walked all the way around the barn.

"Do you think a wild animal could have gotten it?" Hannah asked.

Jemmy shook his head. "Not that mean old thing." Then he looked at her thoughtfully. "Do you think—" he began.

"The British!" cried Hannah at the same moment.

Jemmy turned and raced inside the barn. Hattie! thought Hannah. Oh, what if the British had stolen her too?

But Hattie was in her stall, chewing on a large mouthful of hay. Her patchy brown-and-white face looked as calm and peaceful as always.

Jemmy sighed with relief. "We'd better go tell Mother about the goose," he said.

As they walked back to the shed, something on the fence caught Hannah's eye. Stuffed into a crack was a small scrap of paper.

She pulled it out and unfolded it. On it was written one word: "Sorry."

"Look," she said, holding it out to Jemmy.

"Sorry?" he repeated, scowling. His face turned bright pink with anger. "After stealing our last goose, they say 'Sorry' and that makes it all right?"

It was odd, Hannah agreed. Why would the British leave a note like that?

When they told Mother about the goose, her whole body seemed to sag with disappointment. "Oh my," she said, shaking her head. "Now what shall we do for Ben's homecoming meal?"

It was ruined. Why, Hannah wondered, did this have to happen today of all days? It wasn't fair.

But when Mother looked at the note, her face became thoughtful. "I have a feeling," she said softly.

"What?" asked Hannah, puzzled.

"Whoever took our goose didn't really want to," Mother said. "He only did it because he was hungry. And he felt so bad about stealing that he left us this note."

That made sense to Hannah. Even British soldiers must get hungry. And even the British, she supposed, might feel bad about stealing. Some of them might, anyway.

"It could even have been one of our own soldiers," Rebecca added. "You know how scarce food has been for the Continental Army, especially in the winter. Ben told us about it last year."

It wouldn't be so bad if it were one of their own soldiers, Hannah thought. Oh, she hoped it was!

"What if it were Ben?" Mother asked. "On his way home, so weak and hungry that he didn't know if he could make it. Would we forgive him for stealing a goose? I believe we would."

Hannah nodded. Of course they would. Even Jemmy's face, she saw, was no longer scowling.

"Then we must forgive this poor soldier, whoever he is," Mother said. Straightening her back, she drew herself up with her old energy. "And now we must forget that goose and think of something else to have for Ben's homecoming meal."

"We could stew up one of the hens," Rebecca suggested. She was so much like Mother. Not only did she look like her, but she always knew what to do.

Mother nodded. "I suppose so," she said.

It was disappointing, just an ordinary chicken stew. But at least, Hannah thought, they would have the cider cake.

"The cider cake will make our meal special," she said.

Mother looked at her. Suddenly she was smiling again.

"So it will," she said. "But really we need only one thing to make our meal special. And that is having Ben home with us once more."

Chapter 9

The cider cake, smelling wonderful, was sitting on the table. The stew was keeping warm over glowing coals. Ben's bed was made up near the fire. Everything was ready.

But where were Father and Ben?

Hannah tried to keep her mind on her knitting. Each time she heard something outside, though, she had to jump up and press her nose against the window.

Jonathan was right beside her.

"It's just Mr. Wakefield passing by on the road," he would say sadly.

"It's only the wind," Hannah would sigh with disappointment.

Mother's knitting needles never stopped their *click-click-clicking*. "We have to be patient," she told them.

Dusk came, and they could no longer see out the window.

"Perhaps we should have a bite of supper," Mother suggested.

But even Jemmy, who was always hungry, shook his head.

In the distance a dog barked. Captain? Hannah's heart leaped inside her chest. She and Jonathan ran to the door and peered out. Nothing was there. And though Hannah strained her ears, the sound did not come again.

Then suddenly she heard hoofbeats. A large, dark shadow loomed out of the gray mist, and Jonathan was shouting, "They're here!"

Yes, it really was Ned, with Father on his back and another figure slumped over the horse's neck.

"Jemmy!" called Father. "Come help me get him into the house."

Ben could hardly walk. They had to help him through the door, with Mother by their side, fussing all the while. "Careful, Jemmy. Don't bump the table. Put him down on his bed. That's it, gently now."

Finally, then, Hannah got to see him in the firelight.

She drew in a sharp breath. This could not be her brother Ben! He looked so old. And he seemed to be nothing but knobs of bone with a little skin stretched over. His dark hair was tangled, and a wispy beard covered his face. Only his eyes, large over sunken cheeks, told her that this wasn't a stranger. Ben was really home.

"Mother." He struggled to speak as she covered him with a blanket.

"Hush," she said soothingly. "You are home now. You can rest."

He grasped her hand, and a little smile flickered across his mouth. Then he closed his eyes and was asleep.

This wasn't the homecoming Hannah had imagined. All their fussing over the goose, the cider cake, the special meal—none of that mattered, it turned out. Ben was too tired and sick to care what was in the pot over the fire. And too weak even to lift a spoon to his mouth.

"Where did you find him?" Mother asked in a whisper.

Father stretched his legs closer to the fire. He seemed nearly as tired as Ben. "Wait," he said. "Wait until he wakes up." He too closed his eyes.

No one moved. No one asked for supper. They all just sat silently watching Ben sleep. He looked younger now, Hannah thought, more like himself. She watched his chest moving up and down, up and down, and a wave of thankfulness washed over her. Thanks be to God, she said to herself. He is home.

An hour passed, or maybe two or three. Ben's eyelids fluttered, then opened. For a moment he looked blankly from face to face.

"I—I was having a dream," he stammered. "But it—it is real!"

"Yes," Mother answered. "It is real. You are home, Ben."

A smile spread slowly across his face. "Home," he said hoarsely.

Soon Mother was helping him sit up, and Rebecca was bringing a bowl of broth. Mother fed it to him a spoonful at a time, just as if he were a baby again.

Finally, when he finished and the rest of them had had their stew, Ben began to talk.

"When I saw Captain at the top of that hill," he said, his eyes shining, "I thought I'd gotten myself into heaven for sure."

"Heaven? Hill?" Jonathan frowned in confusion.

"Maybe you'd better start from the beginning, Son," said Father.

"But don't tire yourself," warned Mother. "We needn't hear it all tonight."

"The British set us free," Ben began slowly,

"about a week ago. Carried us in wagons, as so few were strong enough to walk. When they turned us over to the Americans, we were joyful. We were given food and an empty house to sleep in. But the next morning we were left to get home as best we could."

"On foot?" asked Jemmy.

Ben nodded. "I joined with Amos Peabody, as we both were heading in the same direction. We traveled that day, walking and resting and half crawling, as far as Horseneck. We tried to get shelter at a tavern, but they could not take us in. You see, people were afraid of us, afraid of catching smallpox. Children ran away from us as if they were being chased by bears. As we sat there on the stoop of that tavern, who should pass by but Moses."

"And you asked him to go and get Father," Hannah put in.

Ben shook his head. "No, I didn't ask, and he went off without telling us where he was going. We found a rough shelter for the night, but no food. In the morning we set out again. We soon came to a hill. As hard as we tried, we did not have the strength to climb to the top. Finally we lay down, thinking we would die by the side of the road."

Jonathan had tears in his eyes. "Poor Ben," he said softly.

"After resting a bit, I saw that there was a house at the top of the hill. If we could just get to it, I told Amos, perhaps we might get help. On our hands and knees, we began to climb. Looking up again, I saw a large dog at the top of the hill. At first I paid no attention. And then it came to me that it was Captain. I thought I must truly be dying, or dreaming. But a moment later, Father came over the hill."

Ben stopped. He was smiling, but his eyes were wet too.

Hannah could see it all inside her head. Ben struggling so hard to crawl up that hill. Suddenly seeing Captain at the top, and then Father. It must have seemed like a miracle.

They all sat there, smiling and crying and looking at Ben.

"But," said Jonathan, "what happened to Amos?"

"We left him at the house on the hill," answered Ben, "to wait for his family."

"You are tired," Mother said. "You must rest some more."

Ben nodded. He did look tired. So tired that it might take days or even weeks before he had enough rest.

"We made you a cider cake," Hannah told him.

"I smelled it and thought it was part of my dream." Ben tried to smile, but his eyes were closing again. "Thank you, Goosey."

"You will have some tomorrow," Mother promised.

Tomorrow, Hannah thought happily as she settled into her own bed. So many things would happen tomorrow. Ben would bathe and put on new clothes. He would talk and rest and eat cider cake. He would grow stronger.

And she would take care of him. She would nurse him until he was well again. Just like Granny Hannah.

Soon it would really be spring. Ben would be strong and able to help with the house. And maybe Father would let her help more too. Then one day all the neighbors would come for a house-raising. The walls would go up and then the roof. Father would find window glass. And surely by winter they would be living in their new house.

Surely, too, by winter this terrible, long war would be over.

The dying fire popped. Hannah listened to all the other little night noises: breathing and rustles and sighs. With Ben home, they were even more crowded together in the tiny shed. But now it felt cozy. They were all here.

"Welcome home, Ben," she whispered. And she closed her eyes.

Author's Note

The war that Hannah thought would surely be over by the end of 1780 went on much longer. In the last great battle of the Revolution, General Washington's army defeated the British at Yorktown, Virginia, in October 1781. However, peace was not declared until 1783. Finally, after eight years of fighting, America was an independent country.

More than six thousand slaves lived in Connecticut at the time of the Revolution. In Fairfield, most of the wealthier families owned African slaves who served them in the home and as farm workers. Native Americans were also held in slavery. But talk of freedom and the rights of man was in the air, and slowly these ideas came to include the slaves. In 1774, a law was passed that forbade bringing more slaves into the colony. And in 1784, just after the Revolution ended, a new law gradually ended slavery, freeing slaves born in Connecticut when they reached the age of twenty-five.

The place near Fairfield called Horseneck got its name from a peninsula of land that was used as a public horse pasture. The name was changed in the mid-nineteenth century to that of the town in which it was located, Greenwich.

Here is a recipe for Cider Cake that you could try. Be sure always to cook with the help of an adult.

½ cup butter, softened	1 tsp baking soda
1 cup sugar	1 tsp ground cinnamon
2 eggs	¼ tsp ground nutmeg
¾ cup currants	½ tsp salt
2¼ cups flour	1 cup apple cider

Preheat oven to 350°F. Grease a six-cup ring pan or mold. Set out three bowls. In the first one, beat the butter and sugar together until creamy. Add the eggs one at a time, beating each time. In a separate small bowl, coat the currants with ¼ cup of flour. In the third bowl, sift the remaining flour with the other dry ingredients. Add, alternating with the cider, to the butter mixture. Fold in the currants and spoon the mixture into the pan. Bake for 45–60 minutes, or until the cake pulls away from the sides of the pan. Let cool for five minutes, and then invert onto a cooling rack. Use a knife to separate the cake from the sides of the pan if needed. Makes 8–10 servings.

Acknowledgments

My thanks to Barbara Austen, Librarian and Archivist, and William Stansfield of the Fairfield Historical Society for their valuable assistance and advice. The Society also generously granted permission to adapt the recipe for cider cake from their cookbook, *Cooking with Fire*. I am grateful as well to Margaret Vetare of Van Cortlandt Manor and to John Wright and Elizabeth Henderson of Washington's Headquarters Museum, White Plains, New York. And most especially, I am indebted to the recollections of Ichabod Perry, a Fairfield soldier taken prisoner during the American Revolution.

	DATE DUE		

30029001011892
Van Leeuwen, Jean.

F
VAN

Hannah's winter of hope